Little Bear
Brushes His Teeth

Jutta Langreuter and Vera Sobat

The Millbrook Press
Brookfield, Connecticut

One day Mama Bear had a surprise for Little Bear. "It's time to start brushing your teeth after meals just like Mama and Papa," said Mama Bear. "I got you a toothbrush and some toothpaste made just for cubs."

    Now Little Bear had a surprise
for Mama. "I'm not a cub anymore, Mama.
I'm a soldier! I was a soldier all day today with
Bradley and I don't want to brush my teeth," he said.
    "Hmmm," said Mama Bear.

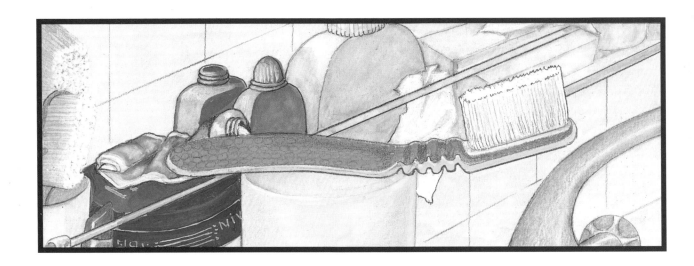

After supper Mama said, "Wash your hands, Little Bear. You are going to brush your teeth. Do you want to squeeze out the toothpaste?"

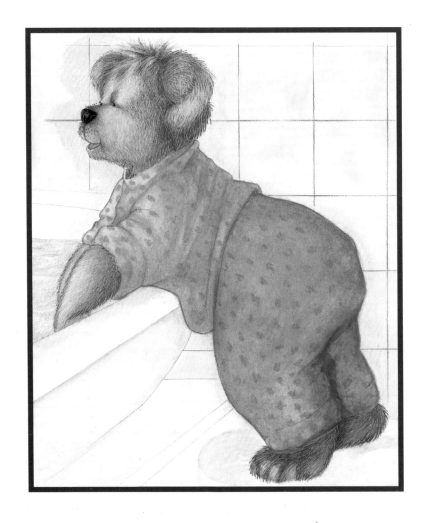

"Sure," said Little Bear, "but I don't want to brush my teeth!"
"I know," said Mama.

"Squeeze carefully, Little Bear. Good job!" said Mama. "Do you want to get your brush wet? Some cubs like it better that way."

"I'm not a cub, Mom. I'm a soldier, and I don't want to...."

"Little Bear," Mama interrupted, "let's try it anyway, OK?"

Little Bear began to brush.

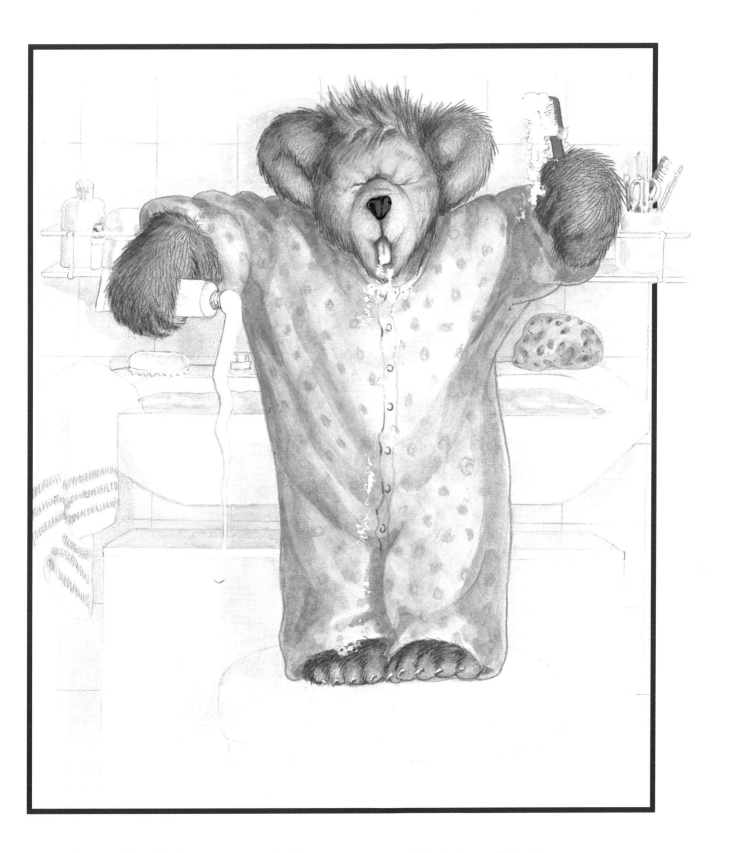

"Yuck!" said Little Bear. "Blech! Ptooey! This is horrible!"

"Look," said Mama Bear when Little Bear calmed down. "Aren't my teeth beautiful? It's because I use my brush and toothpaste every day. You'll get used to it."

"Never!" shouted Little Bear. "And look—my teeth are already beautiful!"

"Yes, they are, Little Bear," said Mama, "and we want them to stay that way. Now watch me," she said.

Mama Bear stood at the sink. She got her brush ready. Then she brushed up and down and back and forth. She rinsed and spit neatly into the sink. "See? My teeth are nice and clean," she said. "Will you try again?"

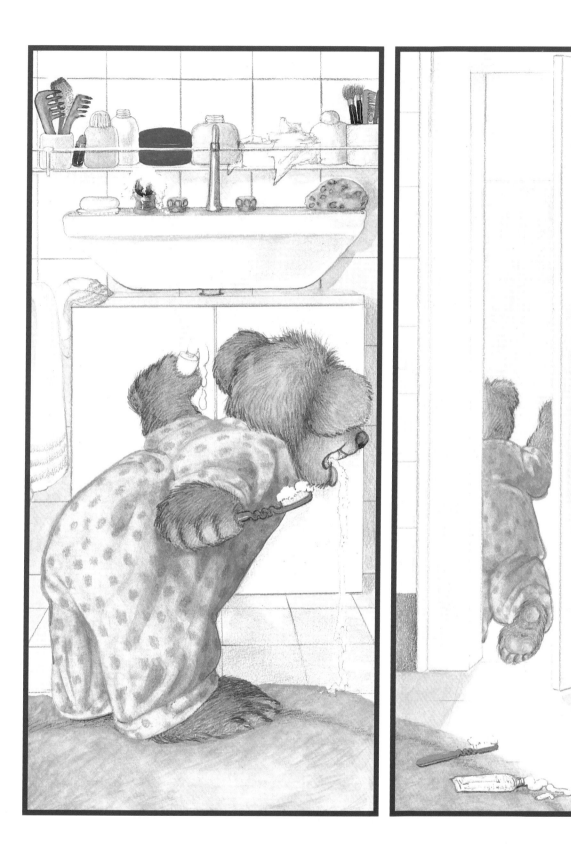

"Your toothpaste must taste a lot better than mine," said Little Bear. But when he started brushing, "Yuck! Double yuck! I do not want to brush my teeth!" Little Bear yelled as he ran down the hall to his room.

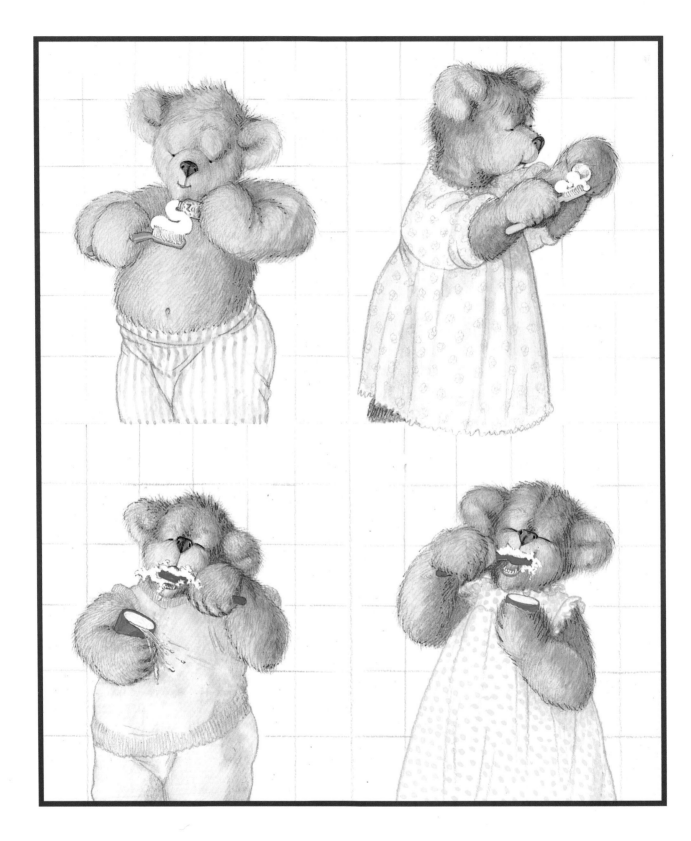

Mama Bear called out, "Little Bear? Do you know what Bradley and Betty are doing right now? They're brushing their teeth. So are Bert and Bertha. All the cubs your age are learning how to brush their teeth."

"Not me," grumbled Little Bear.

Papa Bear was downstairs. "Little Bear won't brush his teeth," said Mama. "Why don't you see if you can talk to him, dear?"

Papa Bear walked upstairs and said, "Come, Little Bear, let me see your new toothbrush."

Little Bear got his new toothbrush, squeezed just the right amount of toothpaste on it, and passed it to his dad. "Well done, Little Bear," said Papa Bear. "You know, I remember the first time I brushed my teeth...."

Little Bear was bandaging Teddy after a battle. He whispered, "Daddy's going to be a while, Teddy. Let's go for supplies!"

Down to the kitchen crept Little Bear, and just as he was helping himself to chocolate cake and honey he heard...

"Little Bear! Where are you?" Uh, oh.

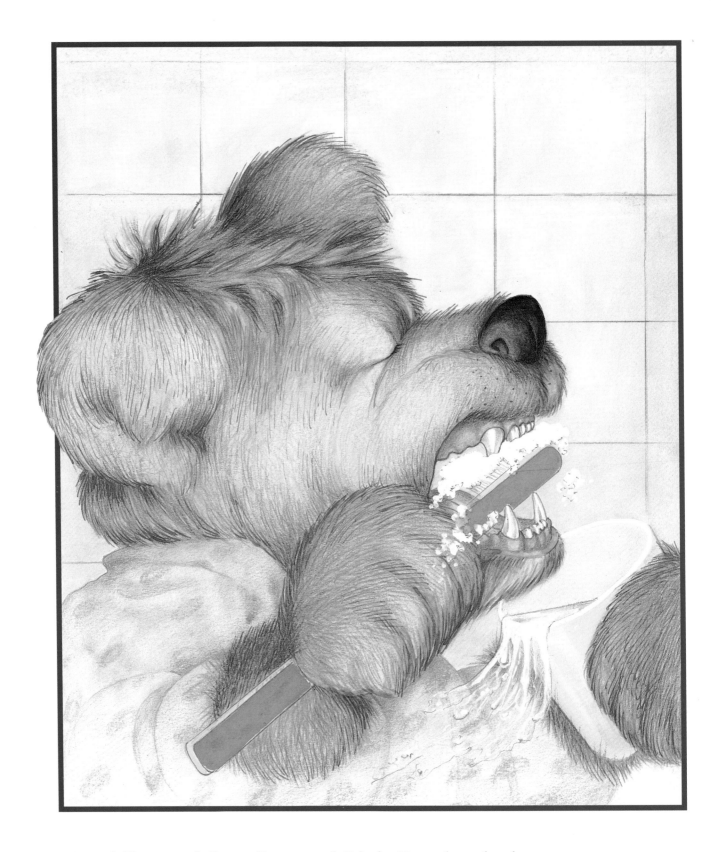

"Brush!" roared Papa Bear, and Little Bear brushed.

"Good boy," said Papa proudly. "That wasn't so bad, was it?
Now go give your Mama a kiss goodnight."

Little Bear snuggled into bed with Mama and showed her his nice, clean teeth. "They feel smooth and clean, don't they, Little Bear?" asked Mama.

"Yup," said Little Bear.

"And you're getting used to the taste of toothpaste, aren't you?"

"Yup," he said.

"And you'll brush carefully after breakfast tomorrow, won't you?"

"Nope," said Little Bear.

"Goodnight, my Little Bear," sighed Mama. Papa snored, fast asleep.

Little Bear was going to be a soldier with a broken arm today.

"Little Bear," called Mama, "come for breakfast! I have a story to tell you."

"Ready!" said Little Bear. He loved Mama's stories.

"OK, my little soldier," said Mama, "this is the story of a battle that goes on every day and you're right in the middle of it."

"I am?" asked Little Bear.

"You are," said Mama. "Now listen."

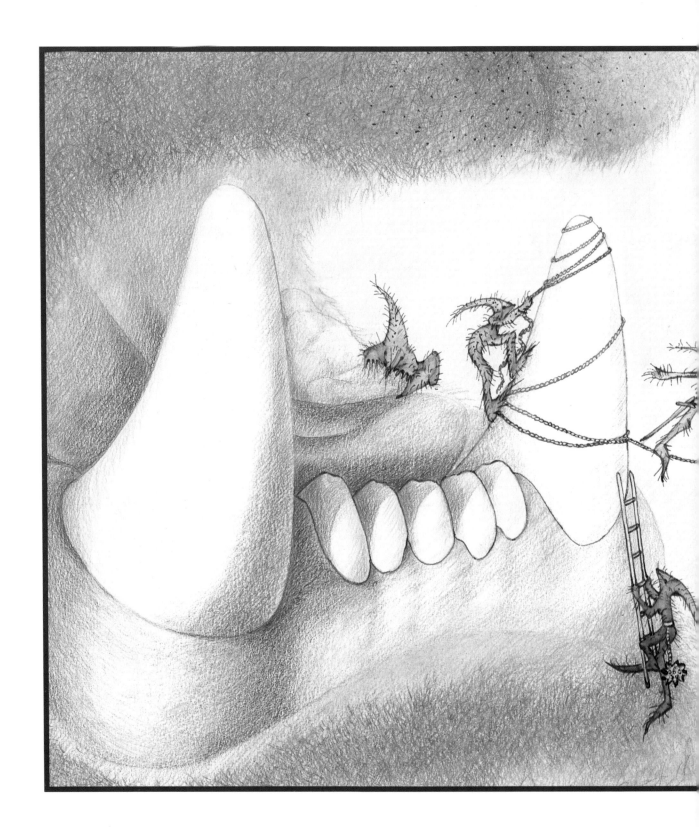

"Every day, after you eat, little bits of food stick to your teeth. Sweets are especially sticky. Those little bits of your food become food for your enemies!"

"What emenies?" asked Little Bear.

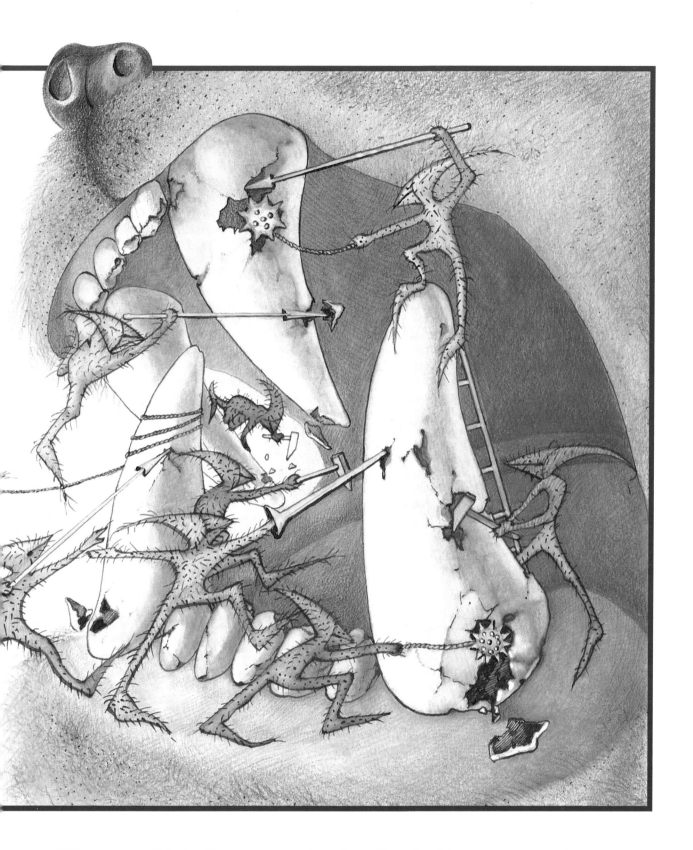

"Enemies, Little Bear, enemies that live inside your mouth. They're called bacteria. They eat the food left on your teeth and make an acid that attacks your teeth. The acid can make holes called cavities that hurt. That's why you've got to brush your teeth—to make sure the bacteria have nothing to eat."

Little Bear gave Mama a big hug and said, "I've got a battle to fight, Mama."

"Yes, you do," said Mama.

Little Bear rushed upstairs to the bathroom where his father was just drying his face. "Papa, guess what!" said Little Bear. "I'm going into battle right now!"

"Is Bradley over already?" groaned Papa.

"No, dear," said Mama Bear, fixing Little Bear's toothbrush, "Little Bear is doing battle for his teeth. We talked about bacteria and cavities this morning and Little Bear is now the Knight of the Shining Teeth."

"Mama," said Little Bear, "pass me my sword!" Mama gave Little Bear his toothbrush and he brushed all around, top and bottom, inside and out.

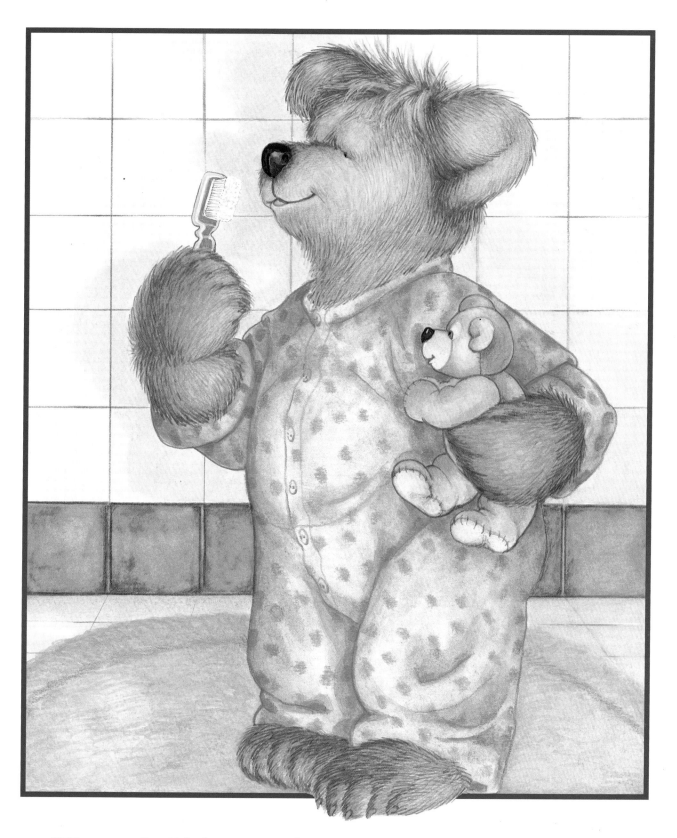

"Hooray for Little Bear!" cheered Mama and Papa Bear.
And Little Bear, with his clean teeth and new toothbrush shouted,
"Hooray for me! I DO want to brush my teeth!"

First published in the United States of America in 1997 by
The Millbrook Press, Inc., 2 Old New Milford Road,
Brookfield, Connecticut   06804

English language text copyright © 1997 The Millbrook Press

Copyright © 1995 arsEdition GmbH, Friedrichstrasse 9,
80801 Munich, Germany

Langreuter, Jutta.
[Kleine Bär muss Zähne putzen. English]
Little Bear brushes his teeth / Jutta Langreuter ;
[illustrated by Vera Sobat].
p. cm.
Summary: Little Bear does not like the taste of his toothpaste
or the feel of his toothbrush, so he does not want to brush his
teeth, until his mother convinces him of how important it is.
ISBN 0-7613-0190-9 (lib. bdg.)   ISBN 0-7613-0230-1 (pbk.)
[1. Teeth—Care and hygiene—Fiction. 2. Parent and child—Fiction.
3. Bears—Fiction. I. Sobat, Vera, ill. II. Title.
PZ7.L2695Ld 1997
[E]—dc20   96-36469   CIP   AC

Printed in Belgium